TALES
FROM
Missouri

TALES FROM *Missouri*

VOL. 1

STANLEY TOWNSEND

CITIOFBOOKS, INC.
3736 Eubank NE Suite A1
Albuquerque, NM 87111-3579
www.citiofbooks.com
Hotline: 1 (877) 389-2759
Fax: 1 (505) 930-7244

Ordering Information:
Quantity sales. Special discounts are available on quantity purchases by corporations, associations, and others. For details, contact the publisher at the address above.

Printed in the United States of America.

| ISBN-13: | Softcover | 979-8-89391-497-9 |
| | eBook | 979-8-89391-498-6 |

Library of Congress Control Number: 2024927092

Table of Contents

A New Amour

You are number one in my heart. Yet I will place you on a mountain. For I have so much respect that its above this mountain.
I placed you on today.
Forever a knight I will be in your court. Cause you are a Queen in my world. Furthermore my lady
I have only one wish that success and good things find there way to you. When I do hear of your successes then I will know. It came true and may it stay with you always.

By. Jake S. Townsend
Oct. 13, 2013

A Past Treasure

When ever I see a farm house out in the country!
It reminds me of the past that has filled my mind here.
To a place where everything was simple and good times was a lot in common.
For when we work on the farm it was long and hard.
This work never gets old cause of our love for the simple things out of life.
For if there was a bad day that happens are very seldom indeed. Now that a treasure like a farm goes away.
You will never know what you are losing when a beautiful memory goes away.

By. Jake S. Townsend
Nov. 5, 2013

A Royal Wish

A time ago in the matters of romance, I thought of a new way to say. If I was a knight in your court "My Lady"
Then a "Princess" you shall be called. Always number one and the top of my world.
If I can give my princess just one royal wish to happen!

Here it is.

"May your beauty shine brighter than the sun? Only let it fall to a greater night.
When an Angel will rise to be more beautiful than before: let that angel be you.
All of the greatest things happening to my princess! Only then my wish came thru today".

She was touched and moved by the kind words by her only knight in her court now.

By. Jake S. Townsend
Oct. 14, 2013

All Alone

At night time once more, I begin to dream about my true love. About her voice sounded to me when I last heard her on the phone.
It was the music for my soul needed to listen once more.

To me it was the sound of angel who made time to visit.
For it is her beauty alone, that gives me strength to go for this one thought.

That I am never tired, although I can only have one dream of seeing her alone.
Which will never be forgotten.

By. Jake S. Townsend
Oct. 16, 2013

Alphabet Thoughts

These are set to the first name. That you are thinking about so much. When you say the name next to the good thoughts: it makes a one of a kind.

To. A

You're always on my mind my love.
When I seen your inner beauty coming out.
To see me as I am: then you found out about the sweetness of my heart.
In time that passes by there were days and nights.
Our love wasn't there like we both shared a bitter fruit of bad days.

Then time passes away only to begin healing.
Our love to be under a great sign,
I am so glad to have you in my life and always on my mind.

To. B

You are the greatest love in my life now.
We crossed paths in our adventures of life.
Our destiny was forever changed by the sweet hand of fate.
To forge our hearts as one!
For we always love each other.

To. C

You are the one who is caring so much.
So thoughtful and very kind: if kindness can be measured out.
It won't even come close to you.
Caring and compassion you have for life all around you.
In my eyes here, that makes you more beautiful.
Lot more back in loving: a great person that I want to be.
Your company to me makes me feel so good on the inside.
So much I feel that I want to say this.
I Love You

To. D

So many times that comes into my mind.
That I wanted to say just: three short words to make your day.
I Love You
Deep down in my own way to show: Double the loving; the time spend only out of my love toward you today.

To. E

It's every day that goes by for when I hear your name.
Once more my love: everything stops on me here.
So I can enjoy the company of your presence.
Gathers up all of my love: I have for you.

To. F

For the first thing on my mind: first person to confess all of my love to.
Forever beautiful in my eyes: forever free to believe in love.

To. G

When ever I think all about your name: It is in the greater respect and good over all.
To say this from my own heart I love you so much.
So great is my love for you, giving me hope and inspiration.

To. H

When you came into my life: you have saved me from the road of blues.
That was a lonely highway for anyone to follow.
Then you have saved me in many more ways.
I just wanted to thank you very much for just being yourself.

To. I

You are so incredible to me, yet impossible not to let go.
Your inner beauty does shine so bright.
I will always see a superstar in you.

To. J

You came into my life with a open heart.
A wide open smile that melted me away!
To love a celebrities who are so jealous now.
For they have never come across some one like you.

To. K

Kindness follows you with open arms.
A loving person whom you are to me:
That brings out all the best things.
That I love all about you.

To. L

You are to me a very loving and kind person,
To spend time with for you have a lot to share.
Enjoying life and thanking what it brings to you.
Then you let the world know out loud.
I was the greatest gift over all.

To. M

Since the last time I saw you standing at the corner of my happiness.
I had this one single passion in my heart.
To respect you and loving so much: the person who came to be.
When I got the chance to know you: I found out that you made my life complete.
You were a down to earth person.
Who made the angels smile from above and kept the devil away.
So the best things I want to say about you is.
That I love you

By. Jake S. Townsend
Oct. 21, 2013

To. N

Now and forever our love is to be.
Needing each other for two things in life!
Strength and Support!
That is always welcome so much into our lives.

To. O

A very rare name now in these days because of its chosen by the ones before.
Telling me only one thing that you are so beautiful in my eyes.

To. P

I am sure to say this right from my heart.
Your name is the prettiest name of them all.
Now I say your name out loud.
I will say it with pride.
Then I will say this to you.
I love you

To. Q

A ruler and a part of my world!
Yet you have one the rarest of names known.
A part of me will always respect you,
A part of me will always place my trust in you.
Cause I love you so much now.

To. R

You are ready to take my heart away my love.
By your inner beauty: and greater gifts you are showing me.
That to me places you into the spotlight of my life.
Let the light of our love shine out to the world.
So we can rendezvous to our better days yet to come.

To. S

Just have to say one of many tributes.
To you today: for you are so very special to me.
I do remember about you is standing so tall having pride so high.
Independent and free, that is what I love about you.

To. T

This is my best wishes; I want to say just for you.
My love
Being terrific you are to my eyes.
It is all I ever see, to the first day we meet.
To our better days ahead when: you came into my world and in my life.

To. U

It is another very rare name you have.
Rarer than a blue diamond: in the eyes of others.
Then in my eyes you must be a beautiful person to be.
When you are in my life now and I will always love you just as you are.

To. V

Another very special name that is so beautiful to hear.
When I do say your name it brings a smile from my heart.
To have this honor and knowing someone one like you.
The most beautiful person I know today.
Well it's you that I love.

To. W

When you came into my life: all I can say is wow.
You were so beautiful I was lost for words.
It was because of your beauty that was standing out.
That it was just something I want to say.
Its all about you that I love so much.

To. X

To the highest honor given: for one who holds this name.
You are a leader and a fighter of so many battles.
Making a difference in our world; by the victories you won.
Letting the defeats go by thru the sands of your time.
This is one thing I want to say out of respect.
That I love you

To. Y

Your name is so beautiful and rare that you hold a place into my world.
Cause you are in my mind so much.
When I do hear your name; I want to say it with pride.
It's a treasure that I must hold in my soul.
That I love you so much; respecting the person you are to me.
My Love

To. Z

It is a very rare honor now to hear about your beautiful name.
These words are only just for you my love.
Let me be into your world to comfort and give back only one sweet gift
of no money.
I want to walk with you every day and always listening to your every
word.
Thru the bad days you alone may face, let me be there to listen to you.
For when we are together my love; we will overcome the odds.
Only to be stronger over time; that I love you and giving all my respect.
To this angel who comes for me now in my life.

An Asian Love

Far and Far away west my heart lies upon a love.
Her beauty was a mystery that was driving my hopes and dreams.
To love her so much that the miles away from me!
Never part the thoughts of sending love back onto her.

If she does come unto my home, let her stay with me always.

By. Jake S. Townsend
Oct. 10, 2013

A New Love

She came into my life when I was down in the valley of hard times.
When being in the dumps on my soul was an everyday thing.
At first I didn't want to speak to her, for I had the fear of being place down again.
Then my harden heart begin to melt away at the moment.
I have seen something very special come out before my eyes.
Her hidden beauty and gift's that was making me noticed.

"I have never looked at the color of your eyes.
All I ever seen was the clearness and gentle heart before me."

Yet her hair was flowing like the prairie grass on a warm sunny day.
So soft and gentle: it was very peaceful just to take a picture.
Just to see this beautiful sight once more for my memories.

When she did speak to me, I have surrendered all of myself to her.
For no other voices outside would never come in to interrupt me,

If she ever touches me, I would melt away any hardness that has made me the way I am.

Now I feel at home knowing that my new love has brought heaven down to earth.

I am glad here that my new love has come into my world.

By. Jake S. Townsend
Oct. 11, 2013

Arrival

When my love shows up just in the nick of time!
To save me from another day of the blues that follows.
Every day I am away.

She was filled with adventure and excitement that follow her.
For she was bless with good luck heading my way in loving!
The way she is and always be in my eyes.

By. Jake S. Townsend
Oct. 12, 2013

Away

When the cruel hand of fate cast an evil spell!
That puts me away from my love.
For a time, I will be in darkness and away from the light of love.
I will withdraw deep inside to a light where my memories are.
It is here I begin to renew my strength and courage.

To a place where happiness stays and time stands so still.
Cause when you are in love with another person.
It's a moment where you feel like the richest person over all.
So I am blessed once again to be in love once more.
Having this secret place in my world where my heart will follow.
Where only one knows about this!

By. Jake S. Townsend
Oct. 13, 2013

Beautiful Sunday

It's in the winter on this day.
At just one time anywhere you go it's the most peaceful.
When you walked around and just notice this one thing.

When springtime comes on this Sunday!
The sight's and sounds of new life coming makes it special.

Summer time on this day
Sitting along side a riverbank!
Relaxing by a creek or a lake: feels so good when the outside
heat gets to much for anyone to endure.
Then you will surely say one thing.
"This is a beautiful day".

Autumn sings a song of change that brings out.
The very best of everything and beauty of all this day comes.
Changes in the trees with fall colors outside,

Its like God is setting the fashion trend in making
his day just "awesome".

By. Jake S. Townsend
Oct. 6, 2013

Beautiful Thoughts

In a series of thought's one would say to win a heart

If I can take a picture of you
That picture would be
How beautiful you are to me
For when I hold this only picture of you
Please let it be the very best picture of all

If you came into my life My door would be open
For you to come right in Into my home
To let time spent
Building the best memories of all

If you can measure thoughts
How can you do this
I would measure my thoughts
Like yards away from you
So longer the yard
More I am thinking about you
So If my time is spent just thinking
Let it be on just one thing only
Let my thoughts bring us together
For our dreams to be coming true

If the power of words can move
Then let my words alone
Moved over mountains
Pass over the open plains
Cross over the seas and oceans
Only to divide the doubts and fears
So it can reach you and say
For the words
    I love you

The nights here where I stay
That I have only one dream
    Let it be only you

You seemed to be so real
For when I touch in a dream

It's a moment in time
I will always cherished
When my dream does come true
That is when you are at my side for real

When I hear any word from you
Just even today
I stop on what I am doing and take notice
On how beautiful you really are to me
How special you are
I am so happy here and blessed to have you in my life

For If a day goes by and night time follows my life
There are moments where I stop and just think about you
Hope that you are doing well
It is out of my true love and deep respect I have here
For you is the center of my world

My Darling
Your love for me is the gasoline for my soul to go on
For you fill up my heart with desire when you are with me
To start dreaming of better things to come between us
I will go on knowing that you love me for just being
Myself

My Lady
If your love itself was a power tool
What would that tool be
Let it be a drill set to drive
For you drive me crazy about you
Loving you just the way you are to me

I will say that true love is a treasure
But your love back to me is so rare
For I am with you
It is so priceless
If our love can be checked for wealth and riches
Then your love is the richest one of all

If an Angel came right into my life
Please let it be you
For you have a way to touch my heart with your voice
Then by chance
When I do hear from you on the telephone
　Let it be the sweetest voice of all
　　That will always make my day greater than before.
　　　You can say with an open heart
It's like an Angel touching me today

Merry Christmas

To the one I love
For I do come with just one gift in mind
Cause I haven't much to give this time
Three very special words
That your heart longs and yearns to hear
I Love You

When I see an Angel right before me
I will always see you
When your eyes sparkle and shine
It's better than the stars above
The night time sky
If I had the chance to touch your skin
It's much softer than the clouds above

When ever I kiss your lips
It's sweeter than a strawberry
If every day goes by and I can love and respect you
This is the only thing I want to say for
Its my gift to you

You're Birthday

Please do not think I am a year older and wiser
Instead think of a second Christmas gift for one

If time it stands so ever still
Let it be a picture of the one I love so much
For the most beautiful person
Who makes me wanting to hold this one picture
In my mind

Beautiful Thoughts Part two

These are very short words that mean so much when you hear them for the first time.

Reward

When life does my way and success follows me.
I always give thanks to God.
Then I want to give back onto others my good luck.
Maybe God will bless them as well.

My Own Quest for Love

When I sleigh the dragons of fear and doubt: then I will yield to my new love.
A victory shall be coming today.
So let the party of our love be the very best one of over all.

Gathering
Once in a great while people will come together to speak as one.
To hear the word of God upon all who are listening.

Kindness

It was shared by all and some goes further.
A long way helping make the world a better place.

To a beautiful friend
Who was and always is number one.
In my heart and mind who was always wishing and hoping
for greater things to come my way.

To a special lady
Who has touched my heart, for it was her beauty. That made me listens to her heart.
Just when she speaks to me, I do stop and take notice. That she is an angel talking to me.
I am lucky to have her in my life.

Happiness

When this restless spirit finally stops: at my home for a spell.
Finding peace at last, for if heaven itself was a place like this.
Then I would never want to leave.
When ever I am happy that is I am calm and sitting down.
Just to look back at my my life and enjoy the blessings of this time.

Redemption

In our own ways we will find a path to forgive.
For it will take us on many ways in life.
Under the eyes of our lord who is watching us every day.

Memories

Are the best movies to watch for when we remember?
It's like watching the best show of all.
The bad memories are always thrown out on the curve in life.
Then we always hold on the good.
When I do remember you: Its like the best show of all in my mind.
Always bigger than a five star movie: and yet no price on admission.
To enter: once again and review.

Caring

On a cold day outside, I would give you my only blanket and chicken soup for the soul.
For the words I would say always comes from my heart.
On a rainy day outside, I will share my only umbrella for you to use keeping the rain away.
From messing with such beauty: that is coming from your grace.

Seeing an Angel

From a distant glance, when my tired eyes are weary.
From my long day of work, I see sunshine coming my way.
For it was a very beautiful person who was taking the time out just for me.
That was the wind beneath my wings and giving me so much strength back.

Apart

When fate alone draws upon a cruel sword: It cuts deeper than a first blow on me.
So we are down for a min, now is the time to regroup and gather our inner strength.
To over take the odds: face the challenge of life.
What rises from it is another meaning of love that no one could ever take away.

A New Love
Today out of all of my days in my busy life: I came across a new person in my life.
Just standing in the doorways of my world: For they was bringing such great changes in my time.

Thinking all about you

A day goes out of my busy life here.
Just like any other days that I will take notice.
Some one who is standing out above all of the rest?
To be number one and no other can hold that spot.
I am happy here.
To remember who I love so.

One more amour

Just one more time to think all about you: If I could dream let it be only you again.
When you kiss me on the lips my love: Let the fire of our passion burn our desires ever wild. Open to expand our burning love.

A Special one

Who makes my heart run faster than a race? Bringing only to me excitement at every turn.
That my life will follow, for I see there own beauty shinning thru.
I drive my heart right into the pit bow of my love. Taken notice of from them because they are a star before me!
They have a voice that I will never forget: If they do say 'Hi' to me.
I will crash my heart into the loving eyes to see what is beautiful over all.

Two adventures with my angel

The first one is when I was on my way in life.
She was by my side, for the upcoming adventures we had.
Made the best books of all ever written; just the two of us.

The second adventure begins when she drives me harder to succeed.
For she was so super to me: If her beauty alone can drive me in the right lane of life.
Then it comes from her heart alone.

A New Years Wish new

To begin something and yet so cool: what is my wish today!
I will say out into the open.
All of the things said unto you.
Let me carry out all you ask for the year.
Love and cherish your presence in my life.

Story behind the Silver Dollar

When you receive this gift from me today: it's the highest gift you will get from me.
This gift is from my heart and it means a lot to me. Why I give this to you!
Its like spending time with a friend like you: Investing in memories over time alone.
Starting to build on good things like this dollar you are holding today.
Now you are one hundred percent my true friend who is very close to my heart.

Romance Recipe

You put in a pinch of respect.
Blend in a dash of trust.
Mix both things over time to a mix of good things.
It's the best thing that makes it real good.

Chivalry

When ever you think of it's gone for good.
Well it just finds another way of showing its true self.
From its start: in England during the days of King Arthur.
Merlin the great wizard found a way to keep it going after he was gone.

Slow Dance

If I can do this one dance with the one I love.
Let my only chance be unforgettable.
For it's a memory made and shared between the two of us.
Is something very special that I hope later on in time?
That there will be another dance between me and the one I love so.

Beautiful Day

When I do look around and see for myself.
The natural beauty of Mother Nature outside: When the wind speaks to me. Its like a story I want to hear. So I can stop and let this wind touch me. Then the message will come clear, someone far away is thinking about you.
That's what happens to me here.

Rain fall

When it does come very slow from the sky: there are times the rain pouring.
It will make the most beautiful sound you will ever hear.
If I walk in the rain just to hear the sounds.
That to me is priceless and wonderful.

Thinking of You

When time does stand still like now. That's when I am thinking of you.
I will say a beautiful thought and it goes like this.
----------------------- I hope that you are doing well and being successful in your days there.
So glad that you are not down and out. If you are down and out: needed to be cheered up. There is someone out there who is always be there thinking about you. Please let it be me right here.

Christmas

It's the time of peace and clam all around me. For a minute out of my life, the spirit of this time comes true. Peace on Earth.

Only Star

In the night time sky above: there was only one star shines so bright upon me.
For you became my only star in my life.
From out of my respect to you: you were placed higher in the nighttime sky.
Cause you are brighter than all of the other stars.

25

Beautiful Thoughts three

These very short verses when you say them out.
They are beautiful to hear when you listen to them.

If my thoughts could reach out: let it be out in the night time sky.
While I am here to witness the stars: the only star I will see is you.
For you are so very close to me. I place you even closer.

To______________
	When I come back and visit you. Once more the vision of your beauty
Fills my heart and desire: and the never ending quest of loving you ever more.

To you______________
	When you surprised me, I am so glad to have you as a friend.
If I had the chance to give: only one thing back to you. That is all of my love and my trust in you.

Rain

When it comes falling down to the ground.
Sometimes it's the most beautiful sound you will ever hear.
Yet It can be from a distance a form of a fog.
Then you will know that "There is rain a coming our way".
On a very hot day outside the news of rain will make any ones day.

Only One love

To the one who is so special to me?
When I am thinking about you: then I am only dreaming about you.
If I am near you baby, my only heart goes on with wild desires to love you.
For the way you are to me the one I love.

Admire

Who lovely vision fills my mind with only thoughts of loving her.
For whom she is number one and has a place in my heart.
Number one in my world now always!

A Vision of You

When I place my only vision of you: then my picture will always be clear.
Just to see how beautiful you are to me.
If there was a song: that can play out my feelings.
Please let that song be "Love me Tender".

Then if there was a song: that speaks of my feelings to you.
Let that song be "As long as I have you".

　　For the one
Who took my heart away by her grace alone?
To inspire me to write a thousand books ever more.
I visited this one heavenly angel: her sight and presence.
Ignites my only passion for loving her as she is to me!
Who has taken my world is all I can say.

To the only One

I admire and respect.
My thoughts are now upon you.
In early springtime bloom all around: one thing for sure that my heart
still belongs to you.

Fore ever

In my thoughts of you: It's like the stars at night.
For you is the only one to me.
When I look at a star, I hope its you.
I will be looking to.

Sweets

For the sweetest you are to me.
Far better than sugar alone: the spice you have inside,
Is the sparkle in your eyes?
It's what makes you special to me.

Thinking of Some one close

A friend so far away yet so very close to my own heart.
I wish and hope only the best for her.
I have so much respect and one more thing about her.

I like so much: a friendship that has started between us.
Just hope that never ends here.

Thoughts

If thoughts alone were of power: then my own would be a super power.
Always on full charge for my own ways to love you even more.
If my own thoughts can travel what speed.
Then mine alone would be at the speed of light.
It's my way once more of loving you so much.

When Angels appear

Out of the blue I was surprise by their appearance.
By someone so beautiful, they will always stand out to be number one
to me.

Always a Valentine

When it comes to be thinking about you: coming up new ways in saying.
I love you
So when I do come up a way of thinking here.
It's like the first valentine that never gets old to me.
Which I always love sending this to you.

When a Eagle Flies

There was a time here that I faced change in my life.
So I asked the Great Spirit for guidance.
It was in the winter here and he sends a eagle to fly away from me.
The message was Flying toward your future and leave you past behind.
That message to me has always stayed with me.

To My Love

Whose name is only known to God?
For now in my dream: she does something that is new to me.
That I want to give her: all of my love all way thru the good days and bad.
Then give her my respect for it is for the best.
That our love stays only in our dreams at night.

To my Amour

I had a wish for you. Here is my only wish.
"May you have a good day and never a bad one? If you do have a bad day and it goes away.
Please open your door to let me in. For once I am here let my amour be only just for you.
To lift you up and out away from the bad day you have faced.
Once that is done and the good day is coming back.
Let me hear all about it and then my only wish has come true once more.

My Heart Measured

If hearts can be measure then mine would be super size with kindness all around.
It's so rare that is so very special.
For when someone who is out there who has shared kindness from the heart.
Like mine for every day will be just like Christmas once more.

My Native American princess

Lady who lives in the woods, I will go and find my guide.
Asking for her help and guidance: so that success can follow.
To a better days ahead for me here!
For I will always say: "Thanks to her" in making my day better.

When I see

My princess in my dreams she will always be there for me.
While I am there all of my wishes do come in.
Only one of my greater wishes I have is.
To spend lots of time with you: and hope that this does so true for me.

Beautiful Thoughts four

Short poems when spoken that will carry a punch to the heart and makes you say "WOW"
When they are read out loud.

Romantic Thoughts Five

These are short poems when you read them out in the open are very beautiful to listen.

When I am alone sometimes I will think about some one so special.
For it's always the right time just to be thinking.
In my mind now it's a vision of a beauty that comes from a lady.
Who has caught my heart and soul and I never want to let go.
So what I do see is driving my own desires to love and respect her ever more.
A lady who has a spot in my heart forever!

Sole and Inspiration

It's not the old song that I am thinking of.
But the one person who has caught my eye: to touch my very soul.
Making me so very weak on the inside: that later makes me much stronger.
She has become my inspiration to be a better person over all.
The whole inspiration to respect and love her!
Going on every day just thinking: about her and loving all of the time.
I would see her and say only this.
I Love you for you're always my amour.

My Love dream of today

I will let you know: to say the shortest words is the first thing on my mind.
Second: always giving you my every day gift my time to spend.
For the number one person in my life: for every day would and always be Christmas to me.
Always giving back so: I can receive the best thing of all your love to me.
That is always my dream today.

About Us

A time ago I have meet someone who was nice and cool to be around.
Who later became my partner in life?
So we began our start and faced so many adventures and challenges.
So we work together to overcome and win so many battles and wars.
That's where our memories begin, now many years later.
Both of us look back at that time: As the best years of our lives when we came together as one.

Time in a Bottle

What does it hold inside, if you open it for the first time?
My own bottle of time will hold the first time that I meet you.
For I am reliving the memory: that fills my soul once more.
Enjoying the moment when it became priceless to me.
Then my time in a bottle is gone for now.
Until I will find another one later on.

My very own Quest

If I had only just one quest, then I will tell you about it.
For I am a restless spirit that never rest: yet there are times I want to stop.
One such rare time I did stop and found peace that my heart years for.
Then there was a beautiful lady who's own beauty made me notice the
greatest gift of all.
She became my friend and partner over time alone.
Her eyes sparkle liked the rarest diamonds for God had spent more time
on her.
Then her skin was so smoother, like touching a gentle breeze once more.
For when I kissed her on the lips, It was sweeter that water on me drying
on a warm spring day.
When I touched once more for there was nothing better at this time.
Now my quest has ended for I am in love with an angel.
Only God knows the name for now.

Dreaming

Just another day goes by when I am just dreaming all about you.
In my everlasting dream, that it's having the chance to love you ever
more.
While I here just love you is the most beautiful person. In my life today:
while you are in my center of my world. To me
It means that you're number one in my heart.

One more night

To have a dream of ever lasting love: for it is the passion.
That will drive me crazy in loving you more every day.
When will have are up and downs in life.
Let our love for each other pulls us thru to the best times of all.

Meeting you

When it happens here! I don't know what to say but "Hello".
Just surprise to see you once more: for what have on the inside.
I never want to forget: always and forever beautiful in my eyes.
A shining star to me at the center of my world: so glad that I am meeting you one more time.

When love is found

Onward my journey I shall go to find a place for my restless spirit to rest.
For it was on this day my beloved came to me in this place.
She was on her road in life waiting for the right time.
Then my heart was weakening by her beauty.
So I do stand up and admire with such great respect for this one lady.
Who has forever changed my world: and never be the same.
For without her presence in my life: my restless spirit would stay forever wild and free.
Never to stop once more a beautiful lady: who makes my days so very nice and yet so cool.

Special One

For the one who has touched my heart: who is making my day so very well.
Now I want to give back just three wishes that mean so much to me here.
Fame
        Is the first wish of mine here, May all of your friends you have makes you feel so good.
Have known so many of them in your world now!

Fortune
        Is the second wished of mine that all of your friends you have make you feel richer on the inside where it counts?

Success
        Is the third and last wish of mine and the one that counts the most over all?
When all of these things going in your way, then I will know from here that all of my wishes came true just for you.

When love is found
Onward my journey I shall follow. To a distance shore for my heart to rest once more.

Beautiful Thoughts Six

In a set of short poems that are beautiful to read and to write out.
When they are spoken for the very first time!

Southern Women

What I love and admire about women from Dixie.
For they rebel only to make this world a better place to be.
For they have the smarts well inside that makes them stand out.
Their beauty and grace is another great thing to admire about them.
I yield and give back to them my highest gratitude and deep respect to all.

Northern Women

They keep values that make them special inside. Love and cherish warmth from their hearts.
They will always get and receive the highest respect from me.

Eastern Women

The birthplace of liberty and: their hearts seeking freedom.
From the darkness that sets them down.
Only to give birth: to very strong and independent women.
That yields to me greater respect and grace they will always need.

Western Women

They are the pioneers that I read about and admire their courage so much.
Those greater things must be said about them.
For when I: alone hear about these women adventures.
There stories makes my heart very proud to have known them.

My angel visits me.

I wonder when my day goes along.
I am hoping that my angel will visit me.
It happens here at night time.
In my only dream I have.
I will begin by saying "Hello" to her.
Then she says "Hi" right back to me and begins our visit.

I will say to her your always be my light for me: A guide for my soul to travel on.
Without you into my world I will see nothing but darkness.
Then she says one thing right back to me.
      "WOW'
The words said at this time ensured our love for each other.

Another look at Love

For when the rain is coming down today at times here.
You can say with an open mind.
How does it look at love?

A rainy day tells me how sad you will be.
When I am away from you and not right there for you,

A stormy day outside: with all of the thunder and lighting going on.
Tells me you are so mad at me for all of the errors I have done.
I begin to make amends for my error's done to you and the skies will be clear.

Important day

I remember today like all other days.
Yet this day is so very special to us.
It was the first time we meet.
You changed my world and it will never be the same.
For the memories we begin to build together.
In time makes for rich and wonderful times.
That makes the richest person at this world very jealous.
On they cannot receive.
      For
Our Love started long ago like a seed in the ground of life.
Now it's grown into a wonderful family tree.

Away

When fate cast itself a bad spell: to put us away from our love.
Let our thoughts and prayers overcome this sudden turn.
That had parted us in this way.
Then we begin once more gather our inner strength.
Finding a way to reach thru the worst of times: upon our darkest hour.
To become our finest hour that brings the sunshine thru to our lives ahead.

To My Love

Who is always having a spot into my world?
For she alone brings to me the greatest treasure of all.
Her presence in my life makes me feel whole on the inside.
For the wealth of her love for me: makes the billionaires out there very jealous.
So now we are in love just her and I. That is the greatest treasure of all.

One Day

It was just like all of the other days in my life. Then I began to think here all about you.
So I begin to dream once more about you. For you was the only star. I love you so very much.
The way you talk to me with such greater thoughts of respect shown.
The way you walk away from me with such joy in your heart.
Knowing that I had made you own day shine with pride.
This only dream stays with me always, drives my desires ever more.
To cherish and love you ever day!
You are my passion to inspire my soul to me.
Cause "Baby you are my only sunshine".

For my only angel

Whose own beauty drives me wild, for the chance of loving her even more?
When I do tell her this that romance to me is in two parts.
First part is respect.
For me here is to give back and honor you with this from my heart.
It means a lot to me here and I am never tired of doing this.
Then comes trust
In time this is so earned and then good things happen that are long overdue.
When you do see this from me and begin to return this beautiful thing.
Back to me and when both parts are blended into one.
Now you have the start of romance once more.

Beautiful Thoughts seven

In a series of short poems when read out for the first time.
They are beautiful just to hear once more.

You're Day

Even when you are in heaven, there is a day when I come by and visit you.
Well today is your day that I am not alone visiting you.
For there are so many other people coming by to visit you: on your day.
If respect was ever measured by the masses to cherish the best memories they have of you.
You want to know there is something very beautiful about your day here.
Is that your memory is never forgotten out of respect and love.

Dancing Angel

Whenever in my night time dreams, I see a beautiful lady to me.
Who has become so very special?
In my heart she has become the best thing happening to me now.
It was her inner gift of beauty that was bringing me in.
Just to hear a story of romance and dancing. The she said this that hit home on me.
Romance is a waltz between just you and me.
Passion is a tango between you and me when things are going so well.
Sometimes it can be both things that mean so much between the two of us.
Salsa is for the adventure our hearts are yearning for to increase our love.

Then I had to leave this beautiful dream with my angel only to return tomorrow night.
Have another dance of her choice.

By. Jake S. Townsend
Nov. 5, 2013

Dream girl

How sweet you really are, to think of me so much.
In my mind, we spend together on a enchanted evening.
Just you and I under a star full night.
Then the stars are ours for the taking.
Placing them into our eyes and admiring.
The stars in our eyes for we are in love.
Then we are talking the night away.
    Just
When the daylight comes up very soon!
Our friendship and growing love is shall be stronger over time.

By. Jake S. Townsend
Oct. 19, 2013

Finding My Angel

When ever I shall travel across so many miles in my life: it seems to be so many light years away from where I stop last. For my journey here never ends, then one day I made a stop. Came across a angel who said "Hello". I was stump and speechless on my end here. Her sweet voice was calling me to stay and visit.

Yet she came across a new friend as well that was changing her world also. What I do love about this angel was her warm smile and she was making a place in her world just for me. Today our love begins between two friends with one thing in mind.

Respect for each other and then trust will grow.

I am glad here that I made this stop in my life.

By. Jake S. Townsend
Oct. 28, 2013

41

First Kiss

It came to me by surprise by an Angel who was right there before me.
Her lips were so fine, far better than the finest wines around.
I have ever tasted. Then she spoke to me, that made my heart quiver from her cupids arrow.
That found a way to my lonely heart. Then for a min it weakens me here.
So I gather my strength and return a kiss back at her. It was my first kiss back to my angel.
Before my eyes she was weaken in her heart by a love who return.
A cupid arrow that found a way to her heart as well: then she said "Wow" back to me.
That's what happens when we share this time together.

By. Jake S. Townsend
Oct. 28, 2013

Girl Friend

To the one I admire so much and yield the highest respect and honor to.
For I want to have only one dream of seeing you: once more hoping that it will be for real.
Then my dream ends and I am awaken and forever apart.
Let my thoughts of your beauty stay with me always.
So I can wish you upon a star that you really are to me.
If I am a candle in your eyes, let me be tall and strong and yet gentle to touch.
For my own flame will be gentle to look and a greater light to look upon with loving eyes.
The fire in my eyes cause of this light of love toward you is in my life today.

By. Jake S. Townsend
Oct. 26, 2013

Giving

This is a story about a young couple in love. For one brings out a new way in showing romance toward the other. We meet Andre and Rita Vamone, Andre is a drama teacher at a local school and while Rita worked the second shift at a local restaurant as a waitress. Cause of their working hours they agree to have separate bedrooms for the time being. Even when they are both married, Yet Rita was feeling down and was heading for a round of being depressed.

That she was like working two jobs one is of home and the second the restaurant. She was feeling deep inside that no one loves her. This sets the stage for four days before Sunday in which Andre did the most beautiful and romantic deal for his wife. If it works their romance will take a big bounce upwards.

Wednesday

Andre made an assignment for the class to do one thing and he gave a deadline of Friday to present it. They was going to make a video of a Hollywood award ceremony. There was only going to be one star in accepting the highest honor present. The video was done on time and Andre gave the whole class an A

Thursday

Andre went to a sport shop and placed a rush order for three trophies to be made like a Oscar and have his wife's named engraved on all three. One is for best person over all, Second is most loved by many and third was loved by one.

On Friday

Rita was feeling more depressed and wanted to forget the horrible week she had. Cause saturday night she was going to be taking the night off and wrap herself in a makeover. Andre was in the works of making Sunday morning a surprise that will change Rita forever.

Saturday / Saturday Night

When Rita got done with everything and wanted to just relax and forget the week that went by so slow. She wrapped herself in a robe, hair in curlers and place a charcoal pack on her face. It may appeared that she was black faced to the outside world. But she didn't care at all about being "politically correct ". Just wanted the night to go away!

Sunday Morning

Just when Rita woke up she heard Andre calling her to come into the kitchen. She noticed that I am walking on red carpet. What's happening here as she was walking toward the kitchen. A DVD was playing on the TV in the kitchen and the first words out from the show. "Rita Vamone you just won a Oscar of Love for being the best person over all in the home of Vamone Motion Pictures". At first she was mad as heck, because she was in a mess with her hair in curlers, a charcoal pack on her face that was getting hard and a robe that didn't want to come loose on command. Then the DVD played again and the show announce Rita Vamone you have just won another Oscar of Love. For being loved by so many how do you feel.

Then Andre came to her to present the last Oscar of Love. This was the one that tops them all.

Rita

When God who is above all of us. Took out time to create an Angel that is you. He broke the mold cause you are so special in his loving eyes. To those all around you, If they have something to say back to you. They would say "You are loved "Then the DVD played comments from all the people in Rita's world letting her know how special she really is. Then Rita surrendered to Andre and said to him.

That is the most romantic thing you have ever done bringing Hollywood home to boost our love life. Tonight I am going to give you a beautiful night to remember.

That is how this story ends.

By. Jake S. Townsend
May 14, 2018 Monday
6:58 pm

Giving

To my only love if I can pick the right flower for you.
Let it be the right one just for you.
If I can make your day better; then let me do this every day.
It's my way of giving back.
If I can make you smile by smiling.
Let me smile to you every day.
If I have this chance to give one more thing!
That is every day that goes on to every night that follows.
To love you as you're are to me.
So very special

By. Jake S. Townsend
Oct. 1, 2013

Her Song for Me

My angel came to me today with a song for me to hear. The song was an old time classic by the Righteous Brothers "Unchained Melody". That was one of her all time favorites, when I heard this song for the first time. It bought goose bumps to my skin. For that song stirred up a good feeling in my heart.

Then I had to come in and think of a song for her. That was very beautiful to hear and came up with a new modern classic. The song was "You raised me up by Josh Groban. That one song was my response to her classic. When she heard this for the first time: she went into tears of joy and was moved by my beautiful thinking here.

Our love brings out the best thoughts for each other.

By. Jake S. Townsend
Oct. 28, 2013

Honor

In the time of the ole South.
I am coming to your aid.
My Southern Belle.
When you called my name today.
All I have is an open ear to listen.
Because I want to hear all about.
Your Very own hopes and dreams.
Here from my heart that I am a part of those dreams of yours.
For If I am not part of those dreams of yours.
I will defend and fight so.
The values you have inside.
For its out of love for you.
I will do this for you today.

By. Jake S. Townsend
9-27-2017 Wednesday
5:56pm

Like a Candle

It's a new thing you can say about romance.
When you are holding a candle still!
It is your friend at first.
Strong and firm it has a place now.
All of the very best parts you like now.

Then a flame will start on the candle and it begins to burn.
We are drawn to the flame with so much interest.
The more flames burn away.
More interest we will be drawn to.
     Then
We do have a soft spot and it's always near the top.
A warm and fuzzy feeling at first, if you touch it then you will feel the heat.
Because this very private moment is number one between you and your love.
You keep this secret by covering the flame and protect what really matters.

Then when the time is so right and you show your love.
To the world and its always so bright.
Like a candle that glows.

By. Jake S. Townsend
Oct. 14, 2013

My Dream Girl

Upon my adventure in life over all!
On this day I look back to the horizon of yesterday.
Looking east upon where my thoughts are going.
There she was standing there just ready.
To take my heart away by her beauty alone!

Her eyes of blue were so clear.
I looked into her soul knowing that she was the one.
That had a ticket into my own soul as well.
Yet it was her inner beauty shines brighter than silver.
But greater than gold to me!

So we start off as friends as first in our lives.
Then only good dreams happen between us.
For the day we are together and our dreams coming true.

By. Jake S. Townsend
Oct. 16, 2013

My Dreams

At any time in my life when I alone!
I have dreams that see a window of things to come.
These dreams have never made sense to me.
For when events do happen in my life and dreams do come true.
It scares me right down to my bones.
      Yet
Having this gift is a rare thing and a beautiful part about me.
That my dreams have taken this path and I feel that I am not alone on this.

By. Jake S. Townsend
Oct. 19, 2013

My Far away Angel

Who has been on my mind for very long time?
All of my wishes for her come true.
My first wish is that she has a great day.
That all of the bad days she has faced before" GO AWAY."
Then I will know in my heart that my wish for her has come true.
My second wish for my far away angel.
Is having the chance to see and hear from her again.
When this happens, then I will know from here that my second wish has
come true.
My last wish that I ever want for her is: I want to call her my friend.
Then I will only ask this from her.
That she thinks of me as her friend from there.

By. Jake S. Townsend
Oct. 28, 2013

My lady's Very Own Beauty

Her hair was a one of a kind that stood out way above the rest.
To listen to her voice singing a song fills my heart with joy.
If she asks me to do anything for her within reason!
Then I will do so without asking.
I think of her in the highest point of respect and honor.
Who is someone who is so special in my heart and mind?

By. Jake S. Townsend
Oct. 20, 2013

My love to be

It was her eyes of blue that was so true.
For they reach the sky and an angel she is to me.
If the chance ever came to kiss this angel's lips!
Her lips are the taste of honey that my heart yearns for.
The day will come for me to hear her voice.
For the first time my heart will weaken.
Just to enjoy having this angel on my side.
So the spell of love cast upon me from my true love.
Is one I will enjoy for a very long time?

By. Jake S. Townsend
Oct. 18, 2013

My Song I will play

This number is dedicated
For anyone who is down and need to believe in impossible.
They will hear a song from me that speaks to the all.
Cause it will find a way to reach deep into the soul.
I will call upon a gentle breeze to go thru the trees so slow.
For the notes only thy heart will hear.
It is new and a sound so soft only I can play.
Then I will call the water to move at the right speed.
To play a beautiful sound that is calming.
On the shores of your inner peace just found at this time.
For the chorus I will call upon the sun.
To break thru the clouds of a soul.
Now you look around and see for the first time.
My world thy hands have made out of love for you.
All of us one time will hear this beautiful song.
Did you ever wonder who composed this tune that is ageless.
Always on the number one list to all.
It is GOD

By. Jake S. Townsend
August 2, 2017
6:22 pm

My Wedding

The day I get married with my love, I hope it's on a Sunday.
For to me it will be my happy time over all.
My dreams are coming true.
Spending my life with you is all I ever ask.

In the eyes of other people who admire us on this sweetest day of all.
Who only have just one wish for the best things in life?
Happening to us on this joyous time over all!

Because I am married to you: my angel my heart,
That no money alone will ever part us away!

You became in my eyes: the greatest treasure in my world.
So our memories together will be building only the best.

Then when I look back to the day: I got married.
That day will always be, the best day in my life.

> By. Jake S. Townsend
> Oct. 19, 2013

My World

One time it was empty and alone until you came into my life.
You brought to me a new meaning to live and explore.
All of the wonders God has made with his own hands.
Then you have given me gifts for my soul needed.

You brought me sunshine on my darkest time in my world.
Only to give back meaning once more thanks to you.

Now we share secrets and hopes and dreams for each other.

All because you have came into my world.
That my life here shines brighter than ever.

Thanks to you my love.

By. Jake S. Townsend
Oct.17, 2013

New Love

This is a story set about a young lady's love of a different kind. For we meet Elissa a beautiful lady who had a secret whom she keep very close. To her heart and it was a personal journal on her own soul. Because she never tells a soul about it; and she will defend it with her best friend Senior 357 magum. For she was a very good crack shot at five hits in dead center at fourty-Five feet.
Claiming that her eyes were getting bad.

Well

Most Men would be scared to death to get close to her. Until one such man tried and succeeded in getting close. On her darkest hour in Elissa life, he would be the shinning star in her life. Luis was a man who was well off in wealth but he didn't want to show it off.
Luis would meet Elissa at the restaurant that she was working in as a waitress and she would serve him. Then Luis would give more than thirty percent tip for her.
Then Elissa had the darkest moment in her life when she tried to buy shoes at a mall and encountered a very rude store clerk and Manager. They refused to help her because; her debit card was no good! They seen Luis and got very nervous and then apologized to Elissa. Because Luis paid for the shoes fast and then got both the manager and clerk back into the store. For he let loose of his latino temper in a classy way and both of them took noticed not to make him mad ever again.
Elissa noticed Luis at the store and asked him. "Why did they get nervous when you showed up"! Luis replied "I owned this mall and I don't like to bragg. I am very wealthy and I 've just defended your honor ". Elissa was surprised by this very kind jesture from a man she rarely knows. In a bold move by her she asked Luis for a date and a surprized at that night.
Luis said "Yes on the date and they meet at his house".

That night at Luis home

It started off with a dinner and a quiet evening talking about life and love. Elissa open up about her life and then surrendered to Luis. By a confession of her deepest secret in the matters of romance.
Luis In the right setting I love to bound and gagged for a short time. So I can surrender to my love and make him mine.

Luis said "Prove it "!

Well Elissa did just that bound and gagged herself on valentines day and Luis was shocked and surprized by this bold move. For the presence of a beautiful Latino woman in this state got to him. Then after a short time Luis set her free and they made beautiful love on that night and in the morning. He was wore out and then made a pledge of love to her.

Elissa agree to the pledge and right then they were a happy couple and in year later got married. This is the only time that Elissa made a confession to a new love.

The End

By. Jake S. Townsend
Feb 14, 2018 Wednesday
6:50pm

One Angel

Her name is secret and only you will ever know Heavenly Father.
Cause I need to show and give all my respect to her.
For when I an do visit and see her in all glory.
I've will know in my own heart that you have made this angel.
More beautiful than ever.
When I go away into the sunset of my days here.
I will always remember in my own heart and soul.
One of your beautiful angels that has always makes my day so special.

By. Jake S. Townsend
October 15, 2017
7:32am

One Day

You will come back to me at the right time.
Just to make my day so much better.
From all of the sadness I faced being away from you.
I need you to come into my life once more.

Please tell me all about your day.
The news always brings a smile to me.
Even here the news always makes my day.
    So
We are happy again just to see ourselves together at last.

By. Jake S. Townsend
Oct. 16, 2013

One Lonely Night Ago

I wish that you are here by my side.
To make my night so much better for me!
I do miss your sweetest voice on the telephone.
Your warm and caring smile: that has melted my cold heart.
You let me care of you once again.
    Now
I only am thinking of you.

You have given back to me faith to believe in myself once more.
To stand tall with pride on my side and having independence again!
    Just

When no one is standing by me, here you are always by my side.
    Furthermore
It's making me here a stronger person on the inside and out. My love is
forever in my heart toward you.

By. Jake S. Townsend
Oct. 16, 2013

One Night

If I had just one wish that wish would be this.
Spend one night with you "My Dream girl".
I want to so much to sit down by your side and listen.
To all of your dreams and wishes that fill your heart with such joy.
Then right before my eyes, I told my dream girl my second wish.
She asked me "What is it"!
I want to spend another night with you and hope that it never ends.
For she was touched and moved by this kind wish: I enjoyed your company very much.
Because you have treated me right my love.

By. Jake S. Townsend
Oct. 28, 2013

One Night

It's a set of beautiful thoughts written down. Like for example
"In a one night setting".

Thinking of you

I stop to remember, just to show.
My thoughts are upon your heavenly beauty.
Because God took out more time on you.
Just to make angels so beautiful.
I will always think of you like an angel.
Nothing will ever change my ways here of thinking.

One Night May 23, 2016

When we are both down by life ways on both of us.
It's our faith in Jesus.
That will see us thru the upcoming challenges.
From this time all we can do is look up.

Just having him in our corner.
We will never go down ever again.

One Night May 24, 2016

Renewing Amour

From the cloudy skies of trouble soul.
An angel will apper from nowhere.
Just in time to lift me up from the downess of my lonely heart.
When I am looking up wpon thee with wide open eyes.
For my first time my love for this angel begins today.
When I meet you for the first time.

One Night May 25, 2016

Above and Beyond

Darling
	When your noble deeds to win my hand succeed. I will take notice
from here and give from my heart. This will be my only signal on to you.
That I have notice what you done.

One Night May 26, 2016

How bold is my love.
Cause I look upon to heaven above.
Just to see my angel whom the Lord knows her name.
I asked Jesus who is above all just one thing,
That is to give back onto me a beautiful sunrise.
So I can show my only love.
All of my power.
All of my strength for there is no other way to show.
How much I love her.

One Night May 27, 2016

War Room

Both of us agree to make a war room for prayer.
Since we both turn to God for help with everyday challenges

Passion

When I am with my love today!
I will have passion in my heart to show.
My greatest gifts are unfolded before her eyes.
I wanted to give more than receiving.
     It is
My undying love and respect for this lady.

That has fueled an inner fire in me.
Which has been grown stronger every day that goes by.
For she has given me a greater gift,

By. Jake S. Townsend
Oct. 15, 2013

Return to Chivalry

Now in these modern days; of super fast internet and rush that is life.
There is something lost from all of the madness.
The lost art of Chivalry, but not to me for I still keep this value close to me.

I think of women as queens to my heart.
To given to all the highest point of respect and honor.
They must deserve this from me at all times.

If I ever find my queen, she will touch my heart.
Cause she will have a place to stay,
I will work on many things here, just to have my queen.

She will forever think of me as a very rare gem.
One of a kind but yet still can lose me.
In this adventure called life.

Chivalry is never dead or forgotten to me. I think not for I still remember it so.
My only way of chivalry is, to respect women for whom they are and let them, know how special they are always to me.

By. Jake S. Townsend
Oct. 20, 2013

Romance

You will know it has two parts for both are equal as one.
The first part is always respect.
To show this for whom they are.
The way they speak and walk.
Just to love them for they are to me.

The second part is always trust.
To take what they say to you.
Beliving in them means so much.
Bye having this in your heart you will go very far indeed.

When these two parts are blended into one.
You will go far and gain something very special.
Spending time to build beautiful memories with the one you love.

Shall be stronger in time when you use these two parts of life.

By. Jake S. Townsend
Oct. 20, 2014

Romantic Thoughts Seven

These are beautiful thoughts that are short and sweet
and yet get to the point when they are read for the first time.

Another Dream

When I am away in my night time sleep: I had a new dream.
That I want to share with you: It begins with just you at a picnic on a summer's day.
Seeing the one I love is so beautiful. It was hard for me to believe. I could be dreaming into her eyes.
Being with me was her only dream coming true. While we both are having this same dream.
Both of us agree that we want this never to end. To have one more time this same wish.

When my Angel changed

If she was down by the weather of life: Then she would change to be better than before.
Onward to the highest star she will climb reaching to be number one.
When she is there: she will shine in the greater glory.
If I can do anything for this angel, Please let me be her friend.
When she can turn to: if she is ever blue.

Miss C Eyes

When I look at her eyes: It's like looking at the night time skies.
For she is and always is a star to me: when I look at her eyes once more.
I see the richness of her everlasting beauty.
She is a diamond in my eyes. So some one like her being the way she is.
So very beautiful in my eyes once more!

Birthday

Well another year goes by to my very special day.
When I say "Happy Birthday" to me once more!
Never thinking I am getting older, just getting better like a wine in time.
Is it always that when we get older?
We do mellow out and take life much slower.
So we can enjoy it more. A lot of people sometimes will come and always

wish the best.
Birthdays will always be a second Christmas.
A second chance: to enjoy more things out of life.

      When Visions do come true
So I do travel to another place searching for an adventure for my heart.
For I came across on my way: a beautiful lady from my past.
Who to me was more beautiful than before since the last time I have seen her.
In my eyes she will always have a place in my heart. For if she ever needed a friend.
I will always be there for her. If I ever had the chance to travel again: please let the one vision I have come true. That is when I see you again the only one who has a place in my heart.

Romantic Thoughts

My Christmas wish

Dear Santa

It is only one that will take it all: it's the only wish that comes into my mind.

To hear from the only one that I love upon this special night: so I send to you my only letter.

Hope from here that you are reading this now in the North Pole.

I want to hear from my angel who is so far away. So we can make this one night so very special. That's all I will ever ask from you and If my wish does come true. I just want to say "Thank you from me ". It means so much to me now.

Signed a true love

Dear Santa

I write to you with only one wish of mine. That wish to be is find a way that our love to be. That is the only gift I ever want from you. From my past year, I had some good and some bad that went away just by talk alone. For that had made me feel so much better: overall about life. I make this one promised to you that the New Year will come and a new fire comes inside of me that burns only one flame now. To find a way to bring my love here and let her live with me. I know that we are going to have some good and some bad. That I hope it goes away by talk alone.

Joan's Prayer

Hello Lord

I come to you today to pray
For finding a way to be with my love
For he has given me so much
From his heart is so strong and now he is believing again
In your grace and realizing your strength
Cause he has discovered once more the power that is in you
For IF we are together under your eyes
Let us both praise and give back thanks unto you

AMEN
My Prayer

Hello Lord
 I come to you today to pray
 My only prayer
 For finding a way that I can be with my love
 For she has given me the gift of caring from her only heart
 That she has set out only from me
 I tried in my past to bring her here
 But it didn't worked out and now I do know why
 Cause Lord you wanted me to build a home
 Now that is what I am doing now
 IF the day does come and we are together
 I want to do one thing together with her

 That is give back to you

 Our daily praise and thanks back to you

Power of One Prayer

Heavenly Father

You know me for who I am.
Cause you only see one at this time.
Sometimes strong: sometimes so silent.
You have created me in this way.
Become a leader among people who needed me.
Giving back strength for others that needed this in middle of storms.

Just when life turns a storm toward me and I begin to lose.
What means so much to me and live for now.
For this event in my life breaks even me down.
To a point where you bring into my world "Silence"!

The only sound I begin to hear at this time.

Then you begin to unleash your mighty power into my soul.
Cause you want me to look up and speak from my heart.

Beginning to say words: that begins the change in my life as well. For the words said

Only you will know Heavenly Father.
Now that I said: speak from my heart unto you.
You have listened to me and then begin changes from your home above.
When I hear and see good news that is coming to my world.
Then I begin to wonder and know now that this one prayer of mine.
That had so much power even I have noticed the power that faith has done for me and now I believe in you.

Amen

AMEN

Only Angel

Let it be only one who has understood me and forgive me.
For all of the mistakes I have made today.
Please let this only angel come into my world to stay.

Coming Angel

For a time here in my heart, I had a feeling burning on the inside of my bones.
That an Angel was coming for me: to bring a beautiful gift for me. The gift is her heart and it would become mine.

Yet now
I have kept this feeling on my inside very calm and cool. For I be reminded of my past, when things never been in my way.

IF this Angel do come into my life, She will stay and become a main part of my world.

All I would ever want from her is just one day to spend with her to learn about God and Jesus. Then praise and do my very best here to honor his word.

Now that my life here: will be changing for the better. All thanks to be giving back to my coming angel.

Romantic Versus

    Hoping to win a heart
These are very short words that might work.

To My Love
    If your beauty was a wonderful spell in the books of life,
That has cast a spell upon my weary eyes. Then let your beauty alone cast
a hundred on
  me today

The passion that fills my heart shall give my life ever more and being to
live and love you more.
Just as you're are to me so
Beautiful in my eyes

When I am away from you, my only thoughts kick into overdrive.
Only to show and to give back.
The greatest respect that anyone shall receive

My only wish that I shall ever have
That it comes true today

French Version

To my Mo Cherrie

  It is your beauty that stays in my mind
For you will always be on my mind with a radiant vision of beauty
That will always stand out to be number one

If I can only give you just one thing out of life
It would be lots and lots of amour
Ever day twenty four/ seven
  yet this will be one thing that never goes old with me
Mo Cherrie
My Amour

Romantic Payback

In a series of very short stories that places our couples in a challenge. To pay each other back without going to SEX. For the muti-billionaire Myron Muddle is the guy who placed this wager, for if each couple does this in a thirty day adventure. For over one day out of their busy week they would come to Myron's mansion. For there effort over time, they would get in return $ 20,000 free in the clear and no taxes on this. For if the couple didn't do this wager they would lose this and be out in the running for the money. It was a contest of to win and nothing to lose. Clarence who was Myron right hand man was the monitor and judge for this thirty day challenge over time.
The couples who have took up on this wager.

>Chase and Giselle Strong
>Saul and Salina Angelino
>Jay and Brenda Dawson
>Bruce and Le Chan Marcos
>Francois and Sherrie Dubois

Why Myron did do this challenge and placed it on the four couples. His reason was the fear of DIVORCE among his five best couples who was friends with him. Because Myron was writing a book called "Romantic Payback" and it was to be the very first in a line of books for his new publishing company.

All of the couples agreed to the challenge and made plans to visit Myron's mansion. Once a week of their busy work load they made a point to come in and spend time with each other. Then Myron made it very clear that only one room there was going to be a videotaping and audio going on. For he was in his office just watching: and listening to all of the ideas coming out from all of the couples. Who have decided to take up on this challenge for twenty thousand dollars?

So it begin at Myron's mansion the contest and he made all of the couples signed a contract.
Myron made it very clear that only one room at his mansion was to have videotaping in progress and Clarence was one of the judges. Along side Myron was made the final call.

For over a six month period all of the couples went thru a series of tests of being classy and sharp.

Then Myron set out the rules of the contest.

One there was going to be AT ALL TIMES NO CUSSING OR FOUL WORDS TO BE SAID BY EITHER PARTNER.

Two   NO SEX AT THE MANSION OF ANY FORM
                   IF CAUGHT THEN THE COUPLE WOULD BE OUT
                   OF THE RUNNING AND BE SENT HOME NO MONEY TO BE
                   CHANGING HANDS

Three   NO FIGHTING
                   VERBAL OR PHYSICAL IT WONT BE PUT UP WITH AND THE
                   COUPLE WILL BE SENT HOME

Fou   NO SMOKING OR DRINKING
                   IF A COUPLE IS CAUGHT THEY WILL BE SENT HOME I HAVE
                   NO TOLERANCE TO THAT STUFF

        Then Myron went on to say this.

        If there is more than one couple who wins this wager then the prize money will double and one partner can complete in this contest while the other is there for them. The whole point of the contest is paying each other back what matters the most. From the heart that matters the most. Already some couples didn't like the rules and were quickly let go. Bruce and Le Chan Marcos didn't like the rules and started to make a fuss. By cussing out Myron and that was one thing that Myron did not like and wasn't going to put up with it. Then Myron explained why he was never putting up with CUSSING.

"When I was growing up on the reservation, I had a very deep religious upbringing and keep it to myself. I never forced this on anyone and later it was a big part of my success. If you look into my office and you will see a cross and a bible. Its mine and NO ONE MESS WITH IT! I will fire anyone on the spot who messes with my bible."

Is it not too much to asked from people not to cuss in front of me!

The remaining couples turn and look around and said one thing back to Myron.

        "NO IT'S NOT TOO MUCH TO ASK FROM YOU"

Then Brenda asked Clarence one question. "Did you ever cross your boss Myron"!

Clarence came back and said "YES just one time and I found out about his Native American name".

"Wolverine"
I came in drunk and wanted to pick a fight and with anyone who was there and cusses out Myron and then stared to hit him hard. I am over six feet tall and Myron was way shorter than me. Well Myron kicked my but before I can say "Amen"! Then he forgives me and asked me to stay and never do that again. Since that bad time long ago I am a changed man and now deeply religious just like my boss.

All of the couples agreed not to cuss after hearing Clarence's story.
This happens during the times of Jay and Brenda was dating.

One by one all of the couples were eliminated and even Jay himself was out for his problems in control and Myron caught him. Then sent him out packing and then I was alone. Myron seen my hard luck and rewarded me with the money.

Seeing You

It was our destiny to meet on a Sunday.
This first day of many in more to come!
When I do look and what see about you.
Are many things that will make you day?

Your eyes sparkle like the stars at night.
Your skin is so smooth like a silk dress.
Then your hair is so soft.
So gentle when I touched!
I want to hold this sweet thought once more.

When ever you do speak to me, I am weakening by your love.
For when you call on me, I will surrender all to you.

By. Jake S. Townsend Oct. 19, 2013

Since you been gone

It has been a season of blue moons for me and many months passed by.
We departed from our last adventure together.
Now my days have no meaning anymore.
I miss you so much.
So sad am I that crying in my sleep is a silent tear only God will hear.
    So
Now I am building once again, to be better than before. To rise from my sadness of ashes a new person to be!

That's what I am doing now.

By. Jake S. Townsend
Oct. 19, 2013

Solitude

In the peace and quiet; where some can find happiness at last!
This very elusive thing that is very hard to do.
Some people will go all out in great lengths to find it.

Then there are times here that solitude can be the most horrible thing.
Any one can endure for it will cut you down very hard and have no mercy.

Either way you look at this thing called "Solitude".

Two things in life that have very different meanings as well!

By. Jake S. Townsend
Oct. 20, 2013

Starting Over

To start over when life doesn't go my way!
Going to a place where no has gone before.

I begin to do things in my own way that will set far from others.
That will set me up to be a legend.
To those who will look back; admire my courage and strength.

They will see a hero in the making and some one to be proud of.

By. Jake S. Townsend
Oct. 17, 2013

SUPERSTARS IN MY WORLD

When the outside world may not give you this Highest Honor

Here where I am at.

I alone give this honor to you

Cause
This picture of awesomeness reminds me of GOD's beauty.
That I loved so much and ready to defend.
The honor of your presence in my life.
Let it be known that I will share and give my all to you.
Out of love that will never ends.
Out of love that has a new start when I look upon this
This beautiful photo that has a place.
On my writing desk now always.

By. Jake S. Townsend
Nov. 10, 2019
8:22am Sunday

Surprise

Today out of all of my days here: my love given me all the wishes I ever wan my first thoughts in my head was "It must be a trap".

Then I said out loud "O'll crap at the worst time. For I alone thought once more that I just killed my romance.

Then she tells me that's its O. K.

Then my heart got to feeling better.

So our romantic adventure is going swell and we learn one thing that's true.

Both of us do love surprises.

By. Jake S. Townsend
Oct. 28, 2013

Honor

The Dance

About myself I am a very hard worker who put in a good week.
Who has gain a fortune by my hands alone.
So tonight I will celebrate.
The fruits of my noble deeds have done.
It's a dance where I will go to shine and bring honor.
To a lady who makes time stands still.

Cause of her beauty alone makes this happen for me.

I asked her for a slow dance under the stars shining.
Just for us the magic is happening under the watchfull eyes.
The one above all of us is smiling.
Seeing two people share something beautiful.
They will always remember this one dance.
Even if they part ways.

By. Jake S. Townsend
9-28-2017
Thursday 6:36pm

The Love Coupon

Its a story about a sleezy lawyer who makes a love coupon to win a lady's heart and takes backwater on it.

Now faces justice by not honoring this.

It was a first for this country judge that both the accused who was guilty and a defendant that her motives were questioned. Yet this judge had to make a ruling now.

So our story begins in a courtroom when this lawyer named Dan Weildo was found guilty of fraud and deciet toward Miss Carlina De Vega. The judge sets out punishment for Mr. Weildo that is new to the court. Then he also addresses Miss De Vega too in his ruling. The Judge speaks to Mr. Dan Weildo first, "Sir you are going offline for three days, No cell phone, No internet and no business calls or have clients visit you. If you refuse my order then I will fine you to the extreme and place you in prison for 25 years and you will lose your license to practice law.

Dan choked at what he was hearing from this judge. Then he agree to the terms of this judgment passed down on him. Then the judge addresses Miss De Vega, For three days you are going offline and No cell phone or internet and no visitors came come over and visit with you. You young lady are going to spend quality time with Mr. Dan Weildo in separate quarters of course.

Miss De Vega came back and said. "What happens if I don't go along with your ruling ". The Judge came back and said. "I will dismiss your case against Mr. Weildo "!

Wow that is extreme your honor.

Then the judge explain the very unusual ruling to the court and what happens next.

So he asked both Mr. Dan Weildo and Miss Carlina De Vega to stand before him now.

Both parties will have to spend time together learning from each other for three days. They will stay in the hotel in separate quarters. I asked the court for my own pay to be cut for three days so that my beliefs to be paid over time.

The Love of the Ballet

Why I love to watch this art that has captured a part of my heart.
To see the dancers shine upon a greater stage.
Bringing a story unfold before my eyes thru dance.
If I could say 'Thank You' to a dancer: for a great job and putting in lots of hard work.
For making my day and If I can come back later on.
I would give back to them my respect and my love to all.
Who are the ballet dancers of my world today that brings this art to life?

By. Jake S. Townsend
Oct. 26, 2013

The Lover's Wish Comes True

Tonight of all nights before us: both of us made a wish and hoping that it comes true.
For the music playing on the CD player is just right and the setting was so great.
Then as we begin our adventure the lights went off and the magic begins.
Later when we look back: and realize that all of our wishes did come our way.

By. Jake S. Townsend
Oct. 28, 2013

The Warrior Brittany

In this set of short stories we will find our heroine. In different wars which take her to the limits where she will shine and takes victory in time.

The first war was in a TV Game Show which she has entered in to win. Cause there were a lot of money to be won. Armed with knowledge she was determined to win. She took on the competition having no fear of them.
This lady was on a mission to better herself in time.
So in the end she won a lot of money and took it back home.
She took back respect and honor and no one would ever doubted her again.

The Warrior Joy

In this adventure takes her in a high class hotel. Working as a maid and
sometimes she is placed in the Kitchen. Doing dishes by hand to please a
manager who she named "Cruella". It was upon one special
night
that Joy's life will changed forever.

For it was a glamour night out in the high class hotel. To raise money for
breast cancer research. Then Cruella strike at Joy and placed her down
and said, Your not going to this fun raiser. You have a
mountain
of dishes to do by hand and you need to report to the kitchen right away.

Her so mean remarks fell upon a man who was visiting. He had enough
and
followed Joy to the kitchen. Then Joy seen the mountain of dishes
that
had to be done and started to cry at her darkest hour. Then Joy
daughter
comes to her and says, "I will help you mom"! Joy came back and
said

      No don't want Cruella to come in, I will get it.

      That's when the man came in and spoke to her.
        "She wont be coming in here, I will am sure of this"!

Joy came back and said, Mr. If you can do this I will listen to you,
While
I am doing these dishes. That's when the man called a staff of people and
they
are doing the dishes, while the man and Joy starts to talk.

He begins with a invite, Joy will you and your daughter come
with me to the funraiser. Joy = I have no dress and what is your catch, I
am not
a charity case, I have my pride you know.

The man says "I am paying it forward with an act of kindness from my heart" I am not
after other things because I have honor and respect to you and your daughter. You can keep
the dresses but for one special night you and your daughter are my guests.
       Then
Joy asked "What is your name ", The man comes back and says
"My name is Jake Tuttle and I am the owner of this high class hotel".
I also own
a high class department store. Tonight I am asking for you and your daughter to come
with me to the dance in the main lobby. My own motive and intentions are is. To pay it
forward.

Joy got mad because she wasn't going to be a charity case and wouldn't let her daughter
be one. Then Jake Tuttle got mad and said, "I just wanted for one night to show an act
of kindness and pay it forward."

Joy accepted Jake's invite and he in turned got dresses for both Joy and her daughter.
For when the dance started in the main lobby of the high class motel. Jake was waiting at
the end of the stair well for both Joy and her daughter.

Then Joy and her daughter made their debut and Jake was surprised and he said "WOW"
at the both of them.

Cruella came back while Jake had his back turned and started being mean to Joy.
   By saying mean things out loud and in public.
Jake had enough and looked around "Cruella and told her that she was FIRED"

Cruella came back and said only "Mr. Tuttle can ever fire me" Then she seen the name tag on the guy.

Jake Tuttle
CEO and Head of Tuttle Department store.

Cruella took backwater and left in a hurry, because she had crossed a line of no return.
Meanwhile
Joy and her daughter had a great time at the dance. Then they left and Jake wanted to say
only one thing. "Even warriors like yourself need allies sometimes".
This made Joy feel better
and in time. She and her daughter became friends to this day.

THE END

By Jake S. Townsend
October 21, 2019
Monday 5:37pm

The Winner

In this tale about a young lady who was named Nana. While in the month of december very close to Christmas.

Nana wanted to impress her mother and get something very close and dear.

To her heart a gift that means a lot and now.

She was studying hard for a spelling bee contest at her school.

The prize was a 50 dollar gift card at Wal-Mart.

She worked very hard and was impressing her mother and her new friend.

Then it came to the night, of the spelling bee contest and Nana who was with her mom and

new friend was working on making a prized video of this very special time. For it was Nana

night to shine. Then the contest came down to just Nana and a young boy the

same age as her. Then she lost and the young boy the same age as her won. Nana was

very mad and was very upset. That is when her mom new friend stopped the video and came to her.

What he said to her on that night made an impression that was forever changed Nana.

Nana "Do you believe in the Lord"

Nana comes back and says "Yes I do believe with all of my heart"

The new friend comes back and says "Nana you are always a winner in his eyes".

Because believing in Jesus makes you always a winner and he is happy to see you smile.

Well he just wanted to give you this envelope and he left because, he is so busy now.

Nana opened the envelope and there was not one gift card. There was two gift cards

made out, is for one Nana and one for her mother. That is when Nana was very happy and

her mother was happy as well.

Tonight was very special for Nana and her mother cause they got closer.

She lost the spelling bee contest but she won something greater. For now it was just three a family now.
   The End

By. Jake S. Townsend
October 27, 2019
Sunday 7:59 pm

93

To my Amour

To My Twin Peak's Angel

Who came from the heaven's to land here.
Cause God wanted angels to land at this time.
The place that lift my spirits up from the blues.
That has fallen upon me.
They bring out from the inside.
What makes them so beautiful all over.

Now it's my turn to be the wind beneath the Angel's wings.
Where my Heavenly Father who is always above me.
You tell me that I can only choose one angel.
To say always from my heart and soul.
For I will always give praise and say "Thanks"
Only you will ever know of her name.
The one who has taken my heart.
Just to show me the beauty that lies in her soul is.
Whats set her apart from other angels that landed.
I've have only wish in my mind and that is.
To know this angel just only one step at a time.

By. Jake Stanley Townsend
June 4, 2017 4:39 am

Tribute

A time ago you went away to become a greater star in the sky above.
For if we look upon the nighttime sky we will always find you very high
in our hearts.
Later we do find out that you were special and was one of a kind.
To those who did love you for whom you really are.
At times when you were here with us: you made us laugh.
Cried thru the sad times and let the bad ones fade away!
Only to show deep inside your greater strengths outward.

Now you have become the biggest star in the nighttime sky.
For if we don't ever see you in the sky: it's because you are sharing your
gift to others and answering prayers to those who needed.

By. Jake S. Townsend
November 5, 2013

True Love

I shall walk this road of my life alone.
Searching for my love and hoping one day to be.
Until one day I have found it.
It was the right time that my feelings followed.
Then I said this to myself in silence.

I hope that you are mine until the end of our time.
I will always love you like no one will ever come so close to you.
My love is true and my respect and honor will follow.

Always

By. Jake S. Townsend
Oct. 19, 2013

Two Days

If I only had just two days to spend with my true love!
Let it be the weekend for sure.
In my world, I will say the most the beautiful things about her.
Her eyes sparkle brighter than the rarest diamonds.
It's one of a kind, because God had spent more time on her.
Yet I know that my lady's skin is so smooth to touch.

It feels like gentle breeze on my own skin.
A feeling that never gets tiring on me!

When I touch her lips for a kiss!
The feeling of static electricity over takes me.
In more positive ways to love and cherished her.

Just the way she is and for these two days.
I have with her, I will make it the very best over all.

By. Jake S. Townsend
Oct. 15, 2013

Two Days in November

In two days on this month there are big thanks that we give back.
First day of thanks is Veterans Day

      A day set out to remember all who served this country.
To give them the highest honor and yet deepest respect over all!
For without their duty and sacrifice the second day has no meaning.
Thanksgiving
      Is the second day we say thanks for so many blessings in my life.
There is one more thing I need to always give thanks.
To
      Jesus
      For giving me strength and courage every day, so I can stand tall
with pride.
All of the great things in that makes this month very special.

      For Me

              By. Jake S. Townsend
              Oct. 14, 2013

Until Next Time

We part in the ways of our lives.
Its goodbye for now and then I hope to see you again.
For one more time only to say.

What I wanted to do, but never had the nerve to go for it.
Now I am alone going over my mistakes.
I have made and now living in the streets of regret.

Then I begin to think once more and start on my new thoughts.
Out of love
I will move mountains by thoughts alone.
To reach you at any place or anytime!
Just to see you once more.
Makes all of the effort worth the time doing.

Because seeing you is giving me the strength.
To keep on loving you, until we do meet again.

By. Jake S. Townsend
Oct. 16, 2013

Valentine

There was two beautiful people who was very deep in love.
Together they faced life like climbing up a mountain.
Bound by their comments made to each other.

For when they faced curves along their trail.
It's is of problems out of life.
They will go at it as a team.
Soon they have no more.

Yet one time darkness fell upon their world.
Where both of them are down for a while.
Just
When one of the lover's discovered something new.
Now the greatest act of love unfolds now.

Drawn into finding faith for thr first time.
For reading about God.
Who was in the skies above him.
Looking into this wonder only.
That only he can do.

Reading more into what his only son done for all.
Our lover does one thing today.
Out of love for the other.

When he placed her upon his shoulders.
She asked him "Why am I up here "!

His only answer was this.
Today I accepted Jesus as my lord and savior.

I read about what he has done and never faced darkness ever again.
Why you are upon my shoulders, I wanted you to be first to receive.
His love for you upon this day and forever.
When you have him in your life you will never face darkness alone.

From these beautiful words he just said. Then he placed her back down on the ground.

She hugged him hard and never wanted to let go.
For this gift from his heart was the very best one of all.

By. Jake S. Townsend
Feb. 14, 2016

Visiting You

While my day goes by: sometimes sooth sometimes crazy at times.
I will stop by and visit you.
Even if it is just a day dream I have now!
This dream of mine is just that.
So my dream begins to have a chance once again.
Loving you just as you are sharing a beautiful memory between you and I.
Is the richest memory of all?
I will have with my dream girl.

By. Jake S. Townsend
Oct. 28, 2013

Walking with Angels

One fine day in the Ozarks where I live, I begin to walk outside on a trail near the woods.

I call my home here, just seeing once more for my eyes. The wonders on what God has done before me. I seen a set of footprints on a muddy trail that didn't belong to anyone I have known.

Then I begin to question it, but I didn't pay it a main at all.

Later on when I had gone walking again on a new road, I had seen footprints again. This time it was following me. Looking around my area and I didn't see no one, that was starting to drive me nuts on the inside.

At the spot on my journey, I stop and found peace once more. Then I went walking again and the same thing happens to me. Another set of footprints along my side.

I went to church and talked to the pastor on what was happing to me here. Then he said to me in confidence "You must have an angel walking with you".

That begins to shake me up here and I am started to believe in greater things.

That was far above me here and I asked God "Why there is Angels walking with me"!

There was no answer and it went for a long time without a reply. It was until I hit rock bottom in my life. I surrendered all and placed myself at God's mercy on me,

Then the answer came by an angel who let me know this to me.

If you are down and feeling low: and alone without love. I will send an angel to be walking with you thru these dark times in your life. You won't see them walking but you will feel someone there for you.

When you see footprints then you will know that someone is there just for you.

Just when things do get better for you that is when you will no longer see footprints beside you.

It's because I will call my angel home. After they give back to you strength and renewing your faith in me.

I was moved and touched by these words and I asked the Angel "Who said this"

The only answer I received was God

From that point on in my life, I was forever changed as a person and begin to believe in the power of God.

By. Jake S. Townsend

Nov. 5, 2013

What I do

When my own life has gone nowhere yet it's empty sometimes.
Why it's so lonely for here to bear.
I always work on being right and seldom done wrong.
Yet when I do, I admit to my mistakes and go on.
Striving to be a better person over all!

So many adventures fall on me that will wear me down.
The point that I almost surrender and let darkness comes in!

Now down inside of me, I just can't give up.
I will fall upon my inner strength and begin with a new weapon.
That weapon in my arsenal is Faith.
More powerful than ever and needed so much.

I will pray to the lord and he is watching over me showing that he cares.
On this time in my life it will be getter better for me.

By. Jake S. Townsend
Oct.17, 2013

What I See

Some one very nice who understands me what ever I say!
That is what I admire about you so much.

You bring back to me something special.
The trips down to memory lane and visiting good times and letting the
bad ones fade.
        Now
For every day and night that comes to us.
Let those times be the very best over all.

By. Jake S. Townsend
Oct. 18, 2013

When I hear from you

Your words alone by email or letter sent to me.
Lift my spirits to new place of happiness in my life.
Just to let you know that I have found you once more.

It seems that time has passed on by since we talked.
For it was way too long in keeping touch.
Now I have found you again, I will never let go.
    Cause
You have made me happy just to hear from you.
It is your thought alone that has cheered my spirits up.

By. Jake S. Townsend
Oct. 17, 2013

When I love

It is only you for no one shall come near to my heart.
For I will be loyal and so true that I might be rare!
In these modern times you need something like this.

I will be so loyal and true, because my world is so empty.
Without you at my side making it better for me!
    Then she said this
Darling
        You make my world so special, to make me dream once again.
Cause you have given me this beautiful gift back into my world.

These words had made my day to hear this from her.

By. Jake S. Townsend
Oct. 19, 2013

When I do walk with You

You let me take only one step at a time.
Thou we shall look upon each other.
Thanking GOD for placing us together.
        So
The road we will travel shall be a long road.
For it will have so many curves and hills.

   Here its a lot like life.
Let it be know unto you, It is your presence
In my life. That becomes the greatest treasure of all.

                    By. Jake S. Townsend
                       October 21, 2019
                       Monday 5:14pm

Honor

When you are Down

It's bye a evil force that has no name or mercy on me now.

That brings my spirit down to a point of defeat in my soul.

So I will be calling you now in my worst time of my life.

To help me overcome these odds before thee.

You now changed your own sword into two greatest gifts given by a heavenly father.

Armed with now courage and inner strength.

I am so happy now that you are now in my corner. Cause you have stopped what you

are doing and being there in my time of need.

It's out of love your light for me is breaking thru this darkest times.

Finding a way to lift me up and beyond my present state.

For when victory comes and I am feeling better. I am very thankful to have you in my life.

Cause you bring the greatest honor out of love.

By. Jake S. Townsend
9-26-2017
7:49 pm

Wild Horses

Just to see these beautiful animals running out in the open.
It amazes me so much to enjoy this beautiful sight.
Yet the sounds of them talking and running.
Fills my own heart here: to hear once more.
One of the most beautiful sights and sounds of all who listen!

For when I hear a baby horse: making its sounds in the morning. Fills my own heart with joy that is why I love horses.

By. Jake S. Townsend
Oct. 19, 2013